Friar Sand
Joins the Pilgrims

Adapted by Fang Yuan
from the novel *Journey to the West*
Illustrated by Wang Qizhong and Cao Shuzhi

FOREIGN LANGUAGES PRESS   BEIJING

First Edition 1985

Hard Cover: ISBN 0-8351-1466-X
Paperback: ISBN 0-8351-1467-8

Published by the Foreign Languages Press
24 Baiwanzhuang Road, Beijing, China

Distributed by China International Book Trading Corporation
(Guoji Shudian), P.O. Box 399, Beijing, China

Printed in the People's Republic of China

The Tang Priest Xuanzang (pronounced Sywanzang in two syllables) had set off long ago towards the West to fetch the true scriptures. The first disciple he won was Sun Wukong, the Monkey King of the Mountain of Flowers and Fruit. At Old Gao Village another disciple, Zhu Bajie, or Pig, had joined them. It was a hard journey. They marched all day and rested only at night.

One day a great river, boiling and raging, appeared in front of them. On a stone tablet beside its mighty waves they could read the words FLOWING SANDS RIVER.

"Disciple," the Tang Priest asked Monkey, "why are there no boats on this wide river in front of us?" Monkey sprang into the sky, shaded his eyes with his hand, and took a good look around.

A few minutes later, Monkey returned to the ground and reported, "Master, the river is around three hundred miles wide with big waves, and there are no boats to ferry us over. We're in trouble." Xuanzang frowned and gave a deep sigh.

As it was getting late, Pig kept complaining loudly about how hungry he was. So the Tang Priest told Monkey, "You had better go and beg for some food first. We will stay here on the bank tonight and decide what to do tomorrow."

"Yes," agreed Monkey. He leaped up on a cloud and flew north to a house where he begged for some food.

In a short while Monkey was back with the food. As he had been so quick, Pig said, "Brother, the house where you begged this food can't be far from here. Why don't we spend the night there?" "On my somersault cloud I can cover thirty-six thousand miles with a single leap," Monkey replied. "But that house is at least two thousand miles away."

Pig said, "In that case you can take the master on your back and carry him across the river by cloud with no trouble at all." "You can ride clouds too," retorted Monkey. "Why don't you take the master on your back and fly across the river? You know as well as I do that because he's a human being he's too heavy to carry that way."

As the three of them were about to eat, they heard a roar from the waves as a monstrous ogre emerged from the water. He had matted hair, two staring eyes, nine skulls slung across his body and an enormous staff in his hand. The Tang Priest couldn't help shouting, "How frightful!"

The ogre made for the river bank in a whirlwind and headed straight for the Tang Priest. Sun Wukong at once took Xuanzang in his arms and carried him high up the bank.

Pig jumped to his feet, picked up his rake and struck at the monster. The ogre parried the blow with his staff, and the two of them became locked in a fierce battle.

The ogre and Pig fought for twenty rounds, but neither came out on top. When the Monkey King realized that Pig was not going to win, he couldn't stop himself from joining the fight. He whistled, sprang down to the riverside with his cudgel at the ready and struck at the monster.

When the ogre saw Monkey coming towards him, he knew he had no chance of winning, so quick as lightning he turned and slipped away. Although Monkey pursued the ogre to the river bank and tried to hit him with his cudgel, the monster plunged into the river, where Monkey couldn't follow him, and vanished.

Pig was certain that the ogre would not appear again. He was very frustrated, stamped his feet and said, "Brother, I was fighting very well. The ogre was losing. If we'd fought three or four more rounds I'd have beaten him, but you came and frightened him into disappearing. We'll never find him again."

"Brother, don't be anxious," Monkey replied. "As you were once in charge of the navy in Heaven, you must be a very good swimmer. Go back into the water and fight with him there to lure him out. Once he's out of the water I can help you finish him off."

Pig thought the Monkey King's suggestion was a good idea, so he jumped into the river with his rake in his hand and dived straight to the bottom.

When he couldn't find the ogre anywhere he shouted, "You good-for-nothing monster, come on out and be a man! Try a taste of my rake!" He swung his rake in his hand and hit the water around him loudly.

By now the monster had recovered from his defeat. Hearing someone challenging him to a fight, he had a quick look and saw Pig charging towards him. He picked up his staff and got ready to fight.

Pig and the ogre fought over ten rounds in the water. Then Pig remembered what Monkey had told him to do and pretended that he was giving up. He slunk away. The ogre fell for the trick and ran after him.

When the ogre came to the surface of the water, Pig had already jumped on the
bank and was taunting him, "Have you got the guts to be a man, you evil
monster? Come on up and fight." The ogre shouted back, "You'll never get me up
on the bank as long as Monkey is there to help you against me. If you're strong
enough, come back and fight me in the water."

When the Monkey King saw that the monster was not going to come up on the bank, he felt extremely frustrated and angry. Suddenly he turned a somersault and stretched out his hand to grab the monster, but the ogre saw him in time, plunged back into the water and disappeared.

As Monkey had frightened the ogre away again Pig shouted at him, "You impatient ape, if you'd just waited until I'd got him out you could have cut him off. But now he's back in the water goodness only knows if he'll ever come out again."

Monkey did not know what to do next. The two of them told the Tang Priest about the difficulties they were having with the ogre. "In other words," replied Xuanzang with tears in his eyes, "we may not be able to get across the river." "Don't worry, Master," Monkey assured him. "I'll go to the Southern Sea and ask the Bodhisattva Guanyin to help us."

"There's not a moment to be lost," said the Tang Priest. "Come back as quickly as possible." Then Monkey somersaulted off on his cloud over mountains and rivers. In an instant the Bodhisattva's paradise island of Potaraka in the Southern Sea was in sight.

Sun Wukong landed his cloud outside the Purple Bamboo Grove, where the twenty-four gods came forward to greet him. Monkey said, "My master is in difficulty and has asked me to speak to the Bodhisattva." The gods replied, "Please wait a minute while we tell her you're here."

The Bodhisattva Guanyin was admiring the blossoms in her lotus pool with the Gold Boy and Jade Girl while she heard the report from the twenty-four gods. Then she asked, "Why has he come to see me instead of escorting the Tang Priest to the West?"

Monkey came forward to see the Bodhisattva Guanyin, knelt on the ground and told her the whole story of how the Tang Priest had met the ogre at the Flowing Sands River.

The Bodhisattva told him, "That ogre was once the Jade Emperor's Curtain-Raising General in the Hall of Miraculous Mist. After he smashed a goblet at a Peach Banquet, he was exiled to the Flowing Sands River."

"This ogre causes a lot of trouble at the river," continued Guanyin. "When he is feeling hungry, he comes ashore and eats up woodcutters and fishermen."

"I passed that way once," she went on, "and urged the ogre to mend his ways. I told him he should wait there until a pilgrim comes by on his way to the West. He can make the journey with him. That will make up for all the wicked things he has done."

The Bodhisattva called in her disciple Moksa, produced a red bottle-gourd from her sleeve, and told him how to use it. Then she asked Moksa to go with Sun Wukong to the Flowing Sands River, deal with the ogre, and help the Tang Priest cross the river.

Moksa and the Monkey King said farewell to the Bodhisattva and rode quickly on rosy clouds to the Flowing Sands River. Before long they were in the sky above the river.

The Tang Priest and Zhu Bajie were waiting anxiously on the bank. Suddenly Pig saw two people in the sky. He looked carefully, recognized Monkey and Moksa, and took a few steps forward.

Sun Wukong told the Tang Priest what the Bodhisattva Guanyin had said. "So you will help us to bring this monster under control, Moksa?" Xuanzang said with relief. He was beginning to feel a little better.

Monkey escorted Moksa to the surface of the river and then returned to the bank to protect his master. Moksa then yelled fiercely, "Wujing, Wujing, the pilgrims who are going to fetch the scriptures from the West are here. Why haven't you submitted to them?"

The ogre, who was afraid that the Monkey King would down to fight him, was hiding among the water weeds in the river. But when he heard his Buddhist name called, he realized that this was a message from the Bodhisattva Guanyin.

Now that he was no longer afraid of being attacked, he emerged from the waves. When he saw that the man speaking was Moksa, he hurried to apologize, "Please forgive me for the way I failed to greet you, Your Holiness."

"Why didn't you greet the Tang Priest when he came to the Flowing Sands River?" asked Moksa. "The Tang Priest? Where is he?" asked the ogre. Moksa pointed at Xuanzang and said, "He's that man sitting on the eastern bank."

When the ogre followed Moksa's finger, he saw the Tang Priest beside Pig and Monkey. One of them was carrying a rake, while the other was holding a big cudgel. "Wait a moment," said the ogre. "I'm not going with them. Those two monsters are ferocious."

Moksa reassured him, "Those two are Sun Wukong and Zhu Bajie, two disciples of the Tang Priest. Now that you have been converted by the Bodhisattva, you are all brothers. You have nothing to fear from them. Go ahead and greet your master."

At that, the ogre jumped ashore, knelt before the Tang Priest and said, "Master, please forgive me for attacking your disciples. I want to accompany you to the West to fetch the true scriptures."

Since the ogre seemed very sincere and had been converted by the Bodhisattva, the Tang Priest let him join their pilgrimage party as the third disciple. Wujing bowed to his master again in gratitude. When the Tang Priest saw that he spoke and acted just like a real monk, he gave him another Buddhist name, Friar Sand.

Friar Sand then took off the skulls that were slung around his body and replaced them with a necklace of nine holy beads. Then he tied the nine skulls together with a rope and threw them into the river as Moksa told him to.

Moksa laid the red bottle-gourd that the Bodhisattva had given him on top of the floating skulls and used his magical powers. In a flash a wooden boat appeared in front of them.

The Tang Priest and his disciples boarded the boat. Although the water was very rough, the boat moved smoothly through the waves, just as if they were on dry ground.

In a few minutes the wooden boat brought them safely to the opposite shore.
Moksa landed his cloud, took back the gourd and boat and prepared to return to
Guanyin's paradise in the Southern Sea. The Tang Priest and his disciples bowed
to Moksa in gratitude and continued on their journey to the West.

美猴王丛书

流沙河收沙僧

方　原　改编

王启中　曹淑芝　绘画

★

外文出版社出版

（中国北京百万庄路24号）

人民教育出版社印刷厂印刷

中国国际图书贸易总公司

（中国国际书店）发行

北京399信箱

1984年（16开）第一版

编号：（英）8050—2560

00400　（精）

00300　（平）

88—E—266